published by

National Center for Youth Issues
Practical Guidance Resources
Educators Can Trust

ncyi.org

www.ncyi.org

In loving memory of our "Kim"

National Center for Youth Issues
Practical Guidance Resources
Educators Can Trust

P.O. Box 22185 • Chattanooga, TN 37422-2185 • 423.899.5714 • 866.318.6294 • fax: 423.899.4547
www.ncyi.org

ISBN: 978-1-937870-04-1

© 2012 National Center for Youth Issues, Chattanooga, TN • All rights reserved.

Written by: Julia Cook • Illustrations by: Anita DuFalla • Design by: Phillip W. Rodgers
A special thanks to Kim "Tip" Frank for technical advise and consultation.

Published by National Center for Youth Issues

Softcover

Printed at RR Donnelley • Reynosa, Tamaulipas, Mexico • April 2016

I'm a blueloon.

I'm supposed to be a regular balloon, but I'm just not having fun like the others. I'm kinda dull, and I'm kinda flat. My string is tied up in knots.

I have a case of the **BLUES**... that's why I'm a blueloon. I've felt like this for weeks!

I remember when I used to feel like a regular balloon.

I was round.

I was bright, and I was pretty happy.

I used to have fun playing with the other balloons...they looked up to me.

I even made little kids smile when I let them hold onto my string!

4

Now, I feel different. I just can't seem to float very high.

Sometimes, I can't even get off the ground.

I feel empty.

There are days when I feel like I don't even have enough air inside me to hold up my string.

5

Then, there are a
few days that are

CRAZY DAYS!

I go from blueloon to
"BALLOONY TOON!"

My head fills up with so
much air that I feel like
I'm going to explode!!!

I float really high.

I talk way too much.

I do really strange things...
and then,

I crash!

Some of the other balloons
are worried about me.

Pink tried to lift me up...
but that didn't work.

Green tried to tie
me down...but that
didn't work either.

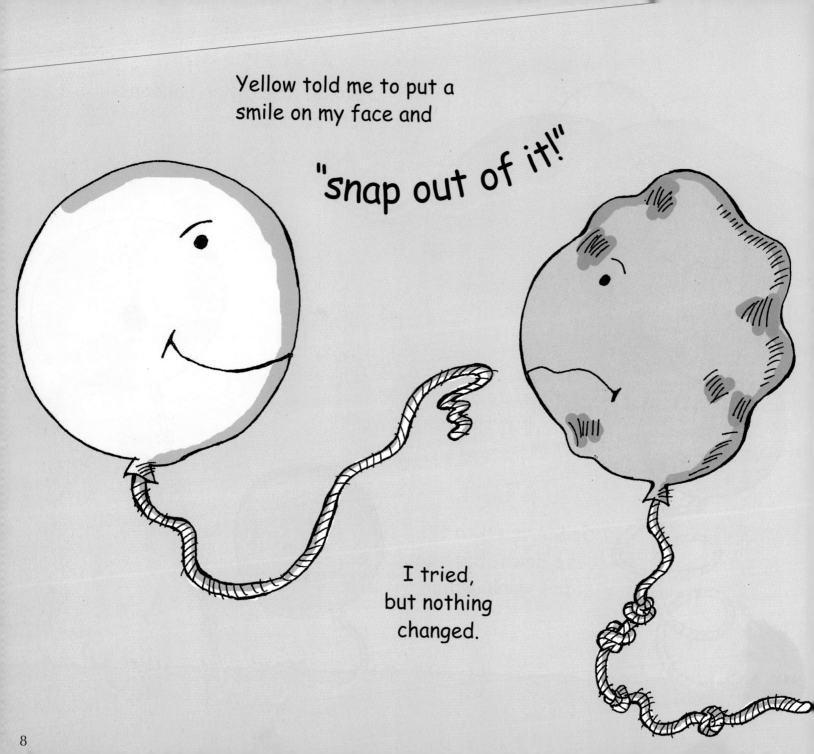

I know there are other balloons
out there who feel like I do, but
I still feel like I'm all alone.

I finally told my mom how I felt.

She gave me a big hug and told me she loved me. Then, she took me to see the wise rock.

"You don't look so good,"
I heard the wise rock say.

"Your string is bent, you have a dent, and you're wrinkly today.

If I didn't know you better,
I'd say that you're depressed.

Are you feeling blue today?
Tell me, how's my guess?"

WISE ROCK

"Actually, I have no idea what's wrong with me," I said. "I just feel blah."

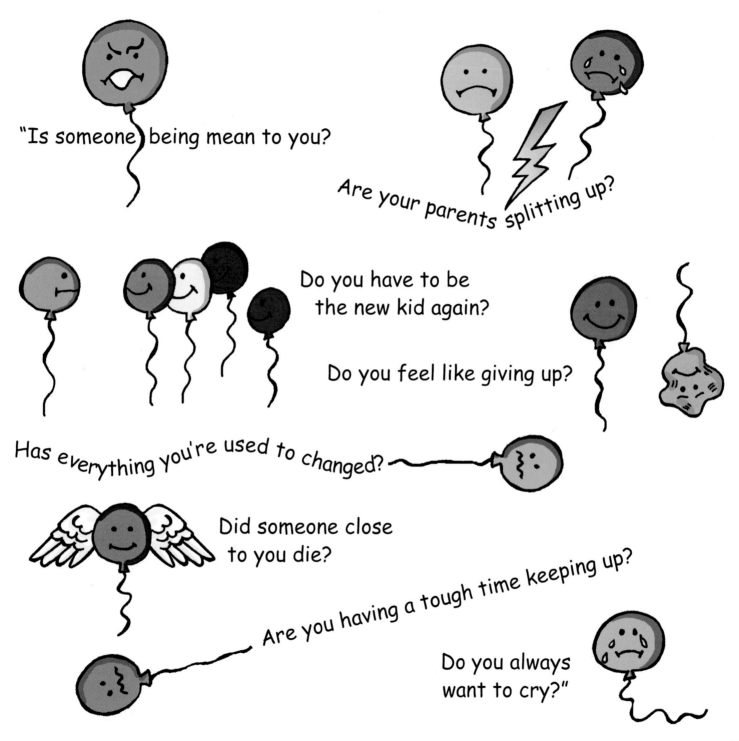

"Is someone being mean to you?

Are your parents splitting up?

Do you have to be the new kid again?

Do you feel like giving up?

Has everything you're used to changed?

Did someone close to you die?

Are you having a tough time keeping up?

Do you always want to cry?"

11

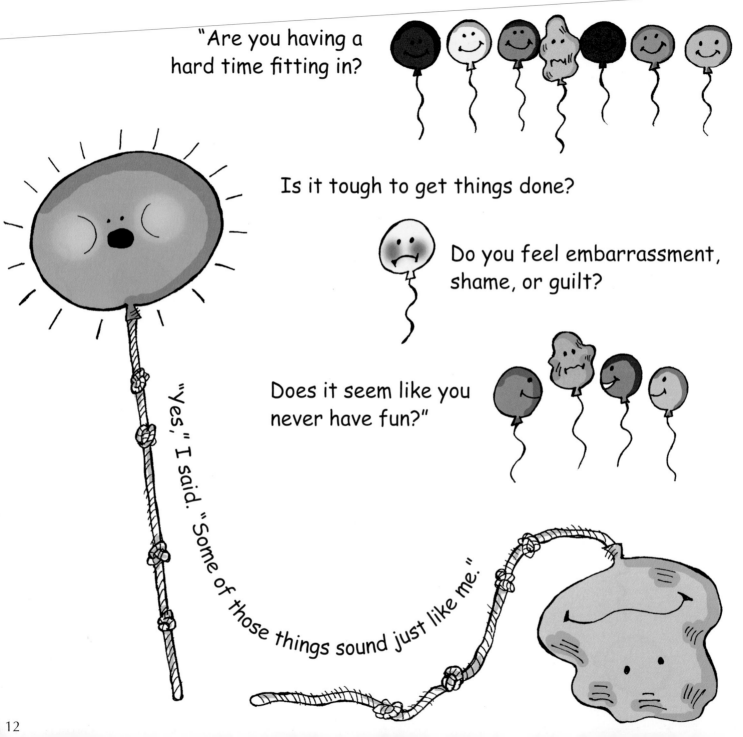

"Are you having a hard time fitting in?

Is it tough to get things done?

Do you feel embarrassment, shame, or guilt?

Does it seem like you never have fun?"

"Yes," I said. "Some of those things sound just like me."

"I understand why you're depressed and
why you feel so sad.

Just hide under me for a little while,
and then you won't feel so bad.

You can talk to me if you want to.
I'll make sure your voice will be heard.

If you don't want to talk, that's OK, too.
You don't have to say a word."

So, I crawled underneath
the wise rock and hid.

WISE ROCK

About 15 minutes later, the rock told me that my hiding time was up.

"Your time to hide is up, my friend.
It's time for you to move on.

You can always come back. I'll always be here to
help you when things go wrong.

You need to go see the balloon doctor.
He'll help you not feel so depressed.

There are also some things you can do for
yourself to help you bounce back to your best."

WISE ROCK

"What can I do?" I asked.

"Well," said the rock, "you can start by deciding that you want to change. Do you?"

WISE ROCK

"Oh yes! I would give anything to have things go back to the way they used to be," I said.

"Well then, you have to learn to believe in yourself."

"Go over and see the balloon doctor.
He'll treat you and give you great care.

He'll make you feel so much better.
He might even give you new air.

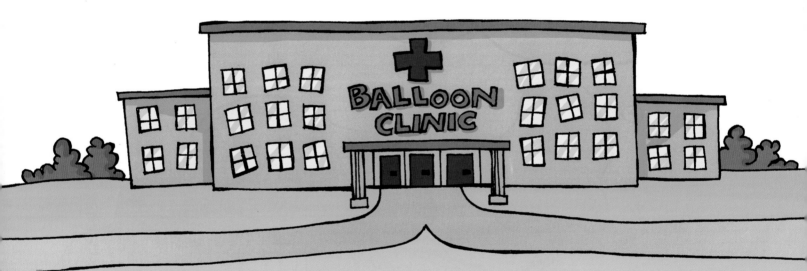

Then come back to me when you're finished.
We'll talk more and figure things out.

I'll teach you some tricks and help you to fix
the things that you're troubled about."

I went to see the balloon doctor.
He was really nice. He checked
me out from the tip of my string
to the top of my head.

Then, he wrote me
out a prescription
for fresh air.

The balloon doctor told me that some balloons
are born with, or somehow develop, a slow leak.
If I keep going flat, he said that I just might
have to keep getting fresh air prescriptions for
the rest of my life.

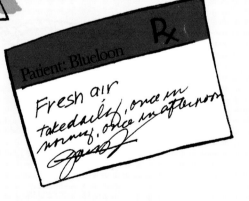

Patient: Blueloon

Rx

Fresh air
take daily, once in
morning, once in afternoon

I got my prescription filled, and then I went back to visit the wise rock.

FRESH AIR

WISE ROCK

"You're looking much better," the rock said to me,
"and you don't have dents anymore.

But your string still has knots, and your face still looks blah.
Your depression is not gone for sure!"

"Let's work on the knots in your string first of all.
Take this pen and this paper and write
all the things that make you feel sad inside
and the things that have messed up your life."

I took hold of the pen and paper,
and I wrote and wrote and wrote.

Each time I wrote something down, one of the
knots in my string came undone. When I had
finished, my string was knot free!

"Now rip up your list and shred it to
bits, then put it inside this jar.

These things won't exactly go away,
but you've shown me how strong you are!"

"I don't feel very strong," I said. "Most of the time,
I feel like I have so much to do that there is no way that I'm going
to be able to get it all done. So, I just don't do anything."

"You have a case of 'Whole Pie Syndrome,'"
the wise rock said.

"You're just like a human who's trying to eat a whole pie
in one sitting instead of just eating one piece at a time."

"Huh???"
"Huh???"

"Make a 'To Do' list of what needs to be done
at the first part of every day.

Do one thing at a time and rest in between.
Your list will show you the way.

Every time you get something done
cross the item off as you go.

You'll feel so good when
your list is complete.

It won't take you long to know..."

"That you can accomplish great things if you try, but you need to believe in yourself.

You have to find hope, and take baby steps, and play with the cards you've been dealt!"

I pulled out a sheet of paper and made my "To Do" list for the next day. When I wrote it all out on paper, my list was a lot shorter than I thought it would be.

"Now think about something that's hard to do,"
the wise rock said to me next.

"Something you think that you'll never get through,
even when you're trying your best."

"Well," I said, "I used to be able to make little
kids smile when I let them hold on to my string.

Now I'm afraid that no matter how hard I try,
I won't be able to float. My string will bend,
and the kids will have to drag me along on the
ground. Then, I might even POP!"

"Close your eyes, Balloon,
and imagine yourself the way
you want to be...
bright, full, and happy
with a very straight string.
Then think,

**'YES! This can
be ME!'**

Tie yourself up to me
and pretend I'm a kid, then
show me what you can do.

Think positive thoughts,
believe in yourself.
Hey, Balloon!!!
Just look at you!!!"

"Wow!" I said.
"I CAN do it!"

WISE ROCK

"Now go on your way, Balloon my friend.

Go back to your life that you know.

Have fun with the others and make a kid smile.

Show everyone how much you've grown."

WISE ROCK

"Take time every day to smell the roses,
and smile at the sun.

You'll start to see that even the little things
can make your life more fun."

"Make sure that you always get enough rest.

Stay away from the air that's not clean.

Be as nice as you can to the other balloons, and exercise your string."

"Like this?" I asked.

"YES! Just like that!!!"

"You'll still have days when you feel blah. It happens to everyone.

But if your blah lasts for over two weeks, and it seems like you never have fun...

If your air starts to leak and you go flat again, you can always come back to your 'rock'.

I'll give you a hug and let you hide out, then I'll take you to go see the doc."

WISE ROCK

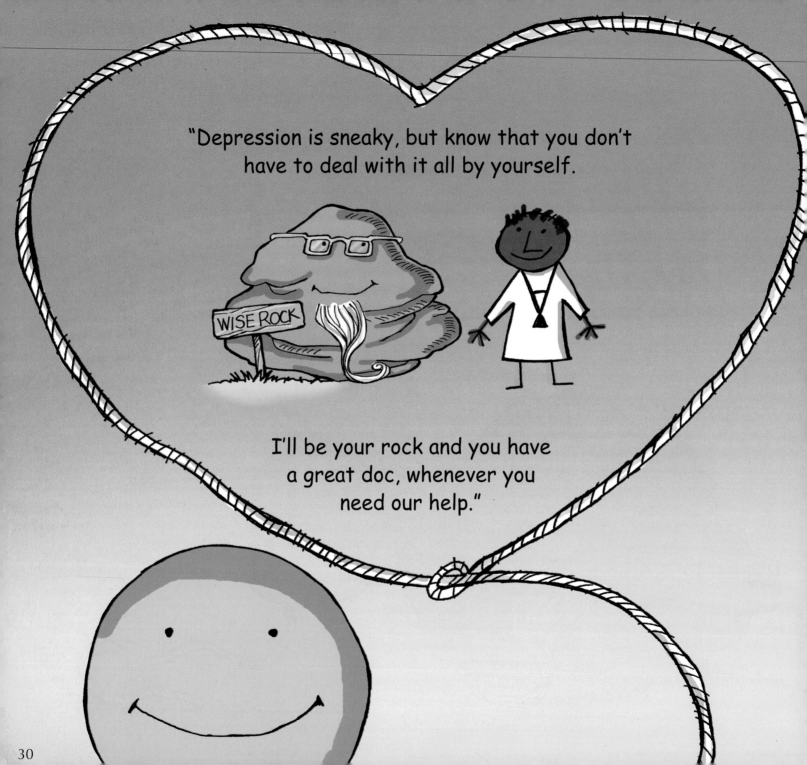

So, I said good bye to the wise rock and ended up having a...

Pretty good day...and a

Pretty good week...and a

Pretty good month...and a

Pretty good year...and a...

A Note to Parents and Educators

Although clinical depression is often thought of as an adult disease, it can affect children as well. Unfortunately, children may not have the maturity to understand what is happening to them, or they may feel powerless to change their situation, so they don't speak up about what they are going through. It is up to adults to be on the lookout for signs of trouble, and recognize when a child needs help.

What to Watch For – The Warning Signs of Depression in Children:

- Sadness, hopelessness, loss of pleasure or interest, anxiety, turmoil (anger outbursts)
- Difficulty organizing thoughts (concentrating), extreme negativity, worthlessness and guilt, helplessness, feelings of isolation, thoughts of suicide
- Changes in appetite or weight, sleep disturbances, sluggishness, agitation
- Avoidance and withdrawal, clingy and demanding behavior, excessive activity, restlessness, self-harm

What to do:

- Don't minimize your child's feelings, and reassure your child that depression is not something to be ashamed about –Some people have a hard time recovering from being sad.
- Work hard to cultivate trust and communication with your child and be aware of the impact your own responses in life are having on your child. You are your child's coping instructor.
- Allow your child the right to feel depressed and teach him that asking for help is ok – If he thinks depression is bad or not ok, he may try to hide his feelings from you.
- Tell your child the truth and give him time to grieve. By being honest, you are allowing your child to work through the pain.
- Pay attention to the length of your child's symptoms. If the symptoms linger for an extended period of time, or if you see severe changes in your child's personality, seek professional help.
- Although suicide in children is rare, it does happen. Take it very seriously if your child says or acts like he wants to die.
- If your child is experiencing frequent signs of depression that last for extended periods of time, it is crucial that you seek professional help. Children who are experiencing signs of depression do not automatically need medication. Many children will respond to therapy alone. If you are uncertain where to seek help, contact your child's school counselor or your family physician for a referral.